SWEET TALES

THE ADVENTURES OF
MISS JADE & BRITT THE KIT

SWEET TALES

THE ADVENTURES OF
MISS JADE & BRITT THE KIT

LAURIE HYMAN

RED SKY PRESENTS

New York

To my loving parents, Celia & Lou Saperstein,
Henrietta & Harry Luchan, and Helen & Marty Hyman.
They all loved and taught me well.

To my husband Micky, who loves me always.

And to all my loving pussycats - nine to date - who
have come into my life, been by my side, and taken care
of me as I cared for them.

A 'Special Thanks' to:

Dorie Riendeau, David Saperstein, Joanne Plotkin,
Mary-Ellen Foster, Catherine Ventura, Belinda Del Pesco,
Heather Wood, Taro Meyers, and Anna Monardo
for the help and guidance they have given me over the years.

Also to my grandkids, Dominick, Emma, Joey,
Ben and Joe, whose love and laughter
are always a source of joy and inspiration.

CONTENTS

TONY NEEDS A FRIEND

CHAPTER ONE

Jade's round green eyes followed Venice the Pigeon as he flew away. The pretty Russian Blue cat didn't know her younger sister, Brittany, was sitting behind her on the terrace of their family's apartment high above New York City.

"What were you and that pigeon talking about?" asked Brittany, an orange and white tabby kitten.

"Nothing that concerns you, Britt," Jade replied, as she turned her attention to the kitten, who had been adopted six months earlier by their humans, Love and Man. The pigeon's news was upsetting and Jade had neither the time nor patience to answer her questions.

"Tell me! Please…" Brittany whined. "He's just an old, fat smelly pigeon. I'm your loyal, fun-loving, very gorgeous own Britt the Kit, loved and adored by all who know me."

"Very funny," Jade playfully growled. "Go away or I'll hurt you. And don't be nasty. Venice is a legend in Manhattan."

"He doesn't look like one."

"You little brat," Jade said, and leaped at the kitten.

Now Brittany was happy. She had Jade's attention. The two cats ran through their spacious sunny apartment. Jade chased Britt over and under furniture, in and out of closets and rooms. They were having a wonderful time when they collided with Man.

"What have we here?" Man said looking down at the cats piled at his feet. Jade stepped away. Brittany meowed and allowed herself to be picked up and hugged. "Was she chasing you? Poor kitten. You can have a treat."

After following them into the kitchen and sharing Brittany's tuna, Jade found a quiet place on the terrace to think and bathe. She jumped onto a pillowed lounge chair, sniffed the air, stretched from head to tail, and circled several times before laying down.

When she was settled, she recalled Venice's words: "There is a boy named Tony. He is frightened and lonely. I don't know how to help him. He is not fond of birds."

While Jade pondered this problem, she used her long pink tongue to wet down one of her front paws. Her silky, blue-grey fur resembled Pussy Willow buds, her favorite nickname. She used the wet paw to make small circles and clean around her mouth and nose. Her eyes opened and closed with the smooth motion. Soon the circles became larger as she moved her paw around her eyes and ears.

Jade thought about the boy's sad circumstances. Tony's father became very sick in the middle of the night a few weeks ago. He was rushed away by ambulance. Jade remembered the night because everyone on their street heard the sirens from the ambulance and police car.

Since that night, Venice told Jade, Tony and his Mom were miserable. "Strangers go in and out of the house. Some bring food. Others stay with Tony when his Mom goes out, and often whisper and sometimes weep. Tony tries to retreat to the backyard or his room but he can't seem to avoid clashing with the grownups."

Jade had felt Venice's anger. "And his Mom has no time for the boy. Not even a smile. She's either out, or yelling, or crying, or talking on the phone. Tony is quite alone and worried about his Dad."

Jade paused and squinted into the sun's light. "He needs a friend," she said softly. I've got to find a way to get to him. I've got to do it without getting caught, or Brittany knowing. I haven't time to satisfy her curiosity."

The smell of coffee drifted onto the terrace. Its scent told Jade milk was around. She jumped from the chair and joined Brittany and Love in the kitchen.

"Good morning, girls," Love said to her cats. Brittany meowed and rubbed against her leg. Jade sat patiently.

"The milk is fresh. You can both have some." She filled two saucers with milk and placed them next to the cats' food bowls.

Brittany took a few licks of the cold white liquid. "You can have mine, Jade. I'm out of here."

As Jade finished the milk, Brittany ran to the terrace.

"Wow! It's a pretty day." She slipped through a tiny opening to the neighbor's adjoining terrace. Once she was on the other side, the kitten was in her own world.

As Brittany looked north, perched on the 18th floor of the Upper East Side building, she was fascinated and frightened by what she saw and heard.

She watched the endless flow of traffic traveling down Second Avenue toward the heart of the city. She followed the sounds of emergency sirens as they raced around the city. Trucks thundered as they moved forward and beeped when they backed up, and there was the continual grinding noise of garbage trucks. She heard children yelling to one another on their way to school. The voices of people filtered upward as they went about their business on the sidewalks below.

Brittany's gaze left the streets and moved to the rooftops of the tenement buildings that stretched for several blocks below her. She saw men working. Teenagers kissed, thinking they couldn't be seen. On a school building, children played atop a screened-in roof.

When the kitten looked higher, her golden eyes squinted at high-rise apartment buildings that soared into the sky, some reaching forty stories. She spotted helicopters and planes as they traveled north along the Hudson River, making a right turn high above Harlem, heading east toward LaGuardia Airport.

"It must be great to fly," she said, watching a bird circle and then fly towards her. It was the same pigeon. She hid behind a potted plant as Venice swooped down and landed on the rail.

"Miss Jade," Venice called. "Please. Come out." His head bobbed up and down nervously. "What can we do for Tony?"

Jade appeared and said with certainty, "I'm coming out."

"But how?" Venice asked.

How, and why? Brittany wondered. She can't get out of here. She laid down quietly and listened.

Jade, not knowing Britt was around, spoke openly. "Rose, our housekeeper will be here soon. I've decided to venture out in the laundry basket."

"Will you be safe, Miss Jade?"

"Time will tell, Venice. Can you wait for me in the backyard of this building?"

"Yes, but…"

"Good. Now, I have to get out without Brittany knowing."

"I don't think you can," said a little voice.

"Venice, why didn't you tell me she was over there?"

"Sorry old friend, I didn't see her." The pigeon poked his head around the divider and spotted the kitten sitting next to the plant. "You must be Britt the Kit. I'm Venice the Pigeon."

"How did you know to call me that?"

"Because it is your nickname." Venice flew down and landed near Brittany. They were the same size.

"If you come closer, I'll attack you," Brittany hissed.

"Will you now?" Venice eyed her carefully.

Brittany suddenly felt timid.

Venice was stunned by the flash of orange that ran past him as Brittany ran to Jade.

"You can't get out," she cried.

"Yes, I can. Now go inside," Jade purred.

"Listen to Miss Jade," said Venice. He tried shooing her into the apartment with his open wings. Brittany arched her back and puffed in protest. Suddenly, the tumblers to the front door lock clicked open.

"It must be Rose!" Jade said.

"Time to fly. I'll be waiting, Miss Jade." Venice disappeared.

"Brittany, will you help me?"

"But I'm scared for you." Brittany touched Jade's nose.

"Well," said Rose, "if that isn't the cutest thing." The cats meowed and ran into their apartment towards the older woman. "How are my girls today?" They purred and rubbed against her leg. "I love you too. We'll play later. I've got work to do." She left the room.

"Brittany, please listen to me! Quick as you can, run to the bedroom, jump onto the bed and stop Rose from taking off the sheets. I need time to hide."

"But Jade, you can't. What will happen if you get hurt? Who's gonna help you?" the kitten cried.

"GO! And don't worry. You can watch me from the bedroom window." Jade patted Brittany's behind. The kitten did as she was told.

When Jade was alone she lowered her head and whispered a prayer. "Please Earth Mother, I need your help and extra power for my journey." Silent and still, she waited for strength and determination to fill her. Slowly she lifted her head and took in as much air as her body could hold, then slowly let it out. "It's time. I do hope this tale has a happy ending."

CHAPTER TWO

When Jade started to move through the apartment she spotted dark colored clothing piled in a wicker laundry basket. She heard Rose laugh and yell at Brittany. Everything was in place.

"Brittany," Rose yelled, "you get out of those blankets. I've got wash to do." The tabby kitten was rolled up in soft ivory sheets. "I can feel you, I'm gonna get you." But Rose came up with a pair of blue jeans.

Brittany peeked out from under the sheets in time to see Jade jump into the laundry basket. A whimper escaped from the kitten's mouth.

"Ah, did I hurt you?" Rose said, picking her up. Brittany enjoyed the comfort of her arms, and then dove back under the covers.

Jade snuggled between two sweatshirts and waited calmly. A moment later she felt more laundry dumped on top of her.

"You in there?" asked Brittany, sniffing around the basket.

"Get away from here!" Jade pleaded.

"What are you sniffing in there, Brittany? You want to go downstairs with me?" Rose asked, as she dropped a heavy container of soap on top of the clothes. Brittany meowed and meowed. Rose bent down and picked up the laundry basket. "Girlfriend, this is heavy." She carried it out the door.

There goes Jade, Brittany thought in despair. I'll probably never see her again.

On the way down, the elevator stopped at the seventh floor. A lady with a Golden Retriever got in. Jade cringed when the dog started to bark at the basket. But when the dog got close enough to sniff the basket, Jade realized it was a friend.

"Quiet, Zoe. Please. I'm hiding," whispered Jade.

"Why, Miss Jade?" asked the dog.

"I'm on a mission."

"Can I help? I will be around the building all day."

"Yes, you can. When you see my Rosie come down again, bark loud five times. That way I'll know it's time to head home."

"Consider it done." The elevator opened and Zoe ran out.

As Rose neared the laundry room Jade became aware of unfamiliar smells and loud sounds that frightened her. Carefully, she nosed away some clothes and looked out. There were large white machines that rattled and shook and spit water when their tops were open. Other machines were hot and smelled sweet.

Fortunately, no one else was in the room. Rose put the basket on a large table, and placed a stack of quarters near the basket. She went to check for an empty washing machine.

Rosie, thought Jade, you're wonderful. You just gave me my way out. The cat used her paw to knock the coins on the floor.

"Now how did that happen?" Rose said as she bent down to pick up the coins. Jade popped out of the basket and quickly looked around the room. When the cat spotted a partially open window high above the table, she leaped to its ledge and escaped. By the time Rose picked up the last quarter, Jade was free.

Jade spotted Venice perched on the branch of a sugar maple tree, cooing along with a melody coming from one of neighborhood windows. She appeared just below him.

"Hello," he called. "Hello, Miss Jade." He swooped down landing next to her. "I'm pleased you got out. Let's go find Tony."

"Give me a moment, Venice. I never had to hide like that to get out before. That darn room is noisy and scary." Jade said.

"You can relax, Miss Jade. You are free now."

"I met Zoe. She'll bark when it's time to come back."

"What about Brittany? Why haven't you told her that you used to come out all the time, before you moved upstairs?"

"I will. She's okay. I told her to watch from the window."

CHAPTER THREE

Brittany settled herself on the sunny windowsill and slowly scanned the adjoining yards that ran the length of the block looking for Jade. From the street no one would know these private green places existed.

Down below, Jade and Venice started across the yard. The sleek blue-grey cat stepped cautiously. The pigeon hopped along. Jade's senses sharpened. Her ears picked up unfamiliar sounds. Strange smells attacked her nose. The rough concrete hurt her soft footpads. She felt skittish and uncomfortable. "Venice, fly ahead. You don't have to stay with me." The bird took flight, happy to be off the ground.

Jade quickened her pace, keeping her head and body low to the ground. As she was about to pass through a hole in an old wood slat fence, Jade looked up toward the apartment building in search of their bedroom window and Brittany. When Jade spotted her sister, she stood proud and determined, in order to show the kitten that she was fine. Brittany was relieved to see her.

A moment later Jade slipped through the small opening and caught up with the pigeon. Venice was waiting on top of a stone wall in the next backyard. "Can you jump up here, Miss Jade?"

"I hope so." Setting her mind to the task, she sat back on her powerful hind legs and used them to spring up easily onto the wall. "There! We have a country home now, Venice, where Britt and I run free all day. It's kept me in shape. Let's go."

They passed through a private yard in the back of a one-family brownstone building, where an English flower garden was in bloom. Jade moved carefully through many different colored flowers, trying not to annoy the bees, who were busy at work. When a few buzzed near her, it took only one hot hiss for them to scatter. She continued unharmed.

The next yard was one of Jade's favorite places. It was a private home that had an authentic Japanese garden. Jade paused and purred. "I wish I had time to stay, but Tony needs me."

"Jade," Venice called. "Come quick. He's here!" The cat responded immediately, moving through the garden, over rocks and in between little statues. She jumped onto a cement Buddha birdbath and leaped to a tree branch that led to Tony's home.

The house had a modest yard. The lawn was neat. There was a swing and slide set at the far end. Jade and Venice sat together in the tree.

"Where is he, Venice?" asked Jade.

"He'll be out in a minute. I saw him inside. He eats lunch out here." Venice added, "If he isn't too unhappy he'll share it with us."

"Good," Jade said, "sharing food would be a good start."

"Look, Miss Jade! There he is!" The sight of the boy made Jade's heart ache. He was about seven years old, with straight light brown hair, and large round blue eyes. He was wearing a baseball cap, an oversized sweatshirt, cuffed blue jeans ripped at the knees, and sneakers and socks. He carried a sandwich, a bag of potato chips, and a glass of milk. Tears ran down his dirty face. He wiped them away with his sleeve.

"Ah, Venice, he's precious, and so unhappy." Jade said.

Tony plunked himself down in the middle of the yard and began to cry.

"You wait here," Jade said to Venice as she started down the tree. She was about to jump to the ground when she spotted a pretty lady by the window.

"That's Tony's Mom," Venice called. The cat waited until the woman moved away. Then Jade jumped onto the grass. The boy saw her at once.

"Go away. I don't have anything for you, cat," Tony said to Jade. "Or you, Mr. Pigeon," he yelled to Venice in the tree.

Jade sat down and studied the boy. He might be tougher than she thought. He opened his potato chips and began to munch. He stared at Jade. She was too pretty not to look at. Jade began to wash her face, using the motion to calm the boy. As Tony watched her, he nibbled at his sandwich.

"That's better", Jade said, watching him. "It's not your food I'm interested in. It's you I want to know, and purr to. I want to make you laugh. Yes, little one, that is why I'm here." The cat stopped washing her face and looked into the boy's eyes. "Open your heart. I have a sweet gift for you. I promise you'll like it." He couldn't look away. He was under her spell.

His tears stopped. His nose stopped running. Jade slowly moved toward him. Tony could hear her purring. Her eyes were so green, beautiful and friendly, that he couldn't wait to touch her.

"You're adorable," Jade purred. "Mmm, that's milk I smell." When she came within arm's length of the boy, she sat down. Tony extended his arm and index finger. It was the way his Dad had taught him to approach animals successfully. Jade stretched her head and sniffed his finger. This was their first greeting. Jade smelled the salt from the potato chips and tuna fish on his finger. She moved a little closer and licked it away.

For Brittany, who watched from the window, their movements appeared to be a gentle dance.

As Venice watched, he knew Jade's magic would help the child. Boldly, the Russian Blue cat approached the small boy and rubbed her head against his knee. Still purring, she allowed him to pet her. Then Jade rested her front paws on his knee and touched her face to his chin. Tony smiled. The cat nudged him with her nose until he laid back and Jade wound up on his chest. He giggled with delight.

"That's it." Jade meowed and sat on his chest. "Let the pain go." Tony sat up, kissed her soft head, and gave her an entire half of his tuna sandwich. She graciously accepted.

"I haven't seen you before," Tony said. He stroked her back while she ate. "I'm glad you're here. My Mom won't let me have a pet of my own 'til I'm older. I'm alone a lot because my Dad's in the hospital. Mom goes to stay with him, but I'm not allowed. I have to be older for that too. I wish he'd come home." Jade meowed several times in agreement.

Tony laughed and held her tight. They played until a dog's bark echoed through the yard and caught Jade's attention. It was time to go. Jade started to leave.

Tony understood and called after her. "Wait. Please. Stay for a few more minutes. Do you want some milk?"

Jade returned to the boy and the milk. Suddenly, the patio door swung open. Tony's mother appeared on the patio.

"What are you doing?" she yelled. "Where did that cat come from? Don't you dare let that animal drink from your glass. What is the matter with you?"

She raced toward the child. Jade froze. "Give me that glass! She screamed. "That animal is full of germs. Give it to me, NOW!"

When Tony didn't move, the woman raised her arm as if to hit the child. Tony ducked, spilling the milk.

Jade hissed, and crouched in an attack position. Venice swooped down and startled the boy's Mother. She backed away. Tony looked up at his Mother. She watched the joy drain from her son's face. His eyes filled with tears and he cried; "Thanks Mom. You just ruined the only fun I've had in weeks." Jade placed herself between the boy and his Mother.

"Tony, I'm so sorry," his Mother said as she approached her son. When Jade hissed again, the woman looked down, first at the cat, then up at the pigeon. "Your friends don't need to protect you from me. I didn't realize you were so unhappy. I've been worried about your Dad and I didn't see your pain." The boy took Jade onto his lap and didn't say a word. "Please, Tony let me make it up to you. We could spend the day together. Would you like me to call Daddy so you can talk to him?" Tony jumped up, released the cat and ran to his mother. "Yes! Please!"

Jade joined Venice in the tree. "Good work, Miss Jade. I heard Zoe barking. We should go."

"I think Tony will be all right for now." Jade said. She looked down at Tony and his Mom and meowed a 'goodbye'. They both smiled and waved to Jade and Venice.

CHAPTER FOUR

"I'd say we were successful. And you, Miss Jade, were wonderful with Tony," Venice cooed. As the cat and bird made their way home, Jade retraced her steps, first passing under the Buddha birdbath in the Japanese garden.

"Thank you," Jade purred. "It's great to be out and about in the city again, Venice. Brittany's a great companion, and I've made new friends in the country. But I miss the adventure of the city and my old friends."

A very handsome black cat was listening to Jade and Venice from the top of the stone wall. His smoky blue eyes were fixed on Jade. At the mention of old friends he began to purr. Jade heard him and looked up.

"Blackie!" Her jade green eyes opened wide. Her ears perked up and her long tail began to sway.

"And they miss you too, my Pussy Willow. My eyes are pleased by the sight of you. We've been apart too long. It won't do, you know. We need to make some plans." He jumped down from the wall and approached her. They touched noses and rubbed against one another. Blackie stayed very close to Jade and acknowledged Venice. "And how are you today, my fine feathered friend?"

"I'm quite well, Blackie. But I'm afraid I have to break up this touching reunion. Jade is running out of time." Venice flew to a nearby tree branch.

"He's right. But we can make plans." Jade paused and looked over her shoulder toward Tony's house. "Blackie, walk me home. I have an idea."

"What are you up to?" he questioned.

"Come with me." She rubbed against him and then, as she walked away, brushed the tip of her tail across his nose.

"Oh no," he sighed. "I know that move. Jade, don't get me involved. I'm too busy. I've got important things to do."

"Ha," laughed Venice. "I can read your mind, Miss Jade. He's the perfect answer for Tony. And you're the only one who could convince him to help. See you both soon." He flew off.

"Who's Tony?" Blackie pranced around and cut Jade off.

"He's a little boy who needs a friend. Please Blackie. He drinks milk." Jade looked deeply into his now laughing blue eyes.

"That's not fair. I can't refuse you." He licked her nose. "I'll check out the kid tomorrow. Let's get you home."

"You'll see," Jade purred. "You two will be great pals." The cats headed back to the laundry room side by side.

"Oh no," cried Jade. "I'm too late. She's in there. Blackie, what am I going to do. She'll see me if I go in now."

"Take it easy. Let me have a look." He peeked in. "It's okay Jade, I know her. She feeds me. How did you get down here?"

"I hid in the laundry basket."

"If I'd known she was yours, I'd have hid in the clothes, and come for a visit a long time ago."

"Really?"

"Sure. Don't you know I'd do anything for you, my Pussy Willow? Now, this is what I want you to do. When you hear her yelling at me, go and hide. And Jade, it's good to be your hero again."

"Blackie, you're the best. Get going," she said, nudging him with her head. They touched and drew in each other's scent.

When Blackie passed through the window his long black tail lingered for a moment around Jade's neck. Once inside, he meowed to let Rose know he was there.

"Well hello there, handsome. It's nice to see you. I didn't bring you any treats today." Rose stood folding large bath towels, and stacking them on the table next to her laundry basket, which was partially filled with folded dark clothes.

Without warning the large black cat leaped from the ledge, and toppled the towels to the floor. "You rotten cat," Rose yelled. "Now why did you do that? You come back here." Blackie ran from the room with Rose hot on his tail.

"He did it!" Jade exclaimed, and quickly moved into the laundry room, and hid safely under the clothes in the basket. Rose returned, picked up the towels, stacked them in the basket, and headed for the elevator. While Jade was being carried down the hallway she heard Blackie purring. She snuggled into the warm clothes with an even warmer heart.

When Rose got to the elevator, a porter was unloading garbage. "Hey, Rose. Can I give you a ride upstairs?"

"Thanks," she said, and got in.

"Well, look who's here," the porter said to the black cat moping around outside the elevator door. "Come on, Blackie. You want a ride?" In an instant the cat was in the elevator.

"Blackie," Jade whispered. "When you said you'd see me home, I didn't know you meant to my door." Blackie sat near the basket, very proud of himself.

After Venice had watched Jade enter the laundry room, he decided to let Brittany know her sister was heading home. He flew to the window where Brittany was waiting.

"Is my sister okay, Venice?" cried Brittany. "Who was that black cat? How's the boy? Where's Jade? When will she be back? Tell me... Please!"

"It's all fine, Britt the Kit. Calm yourself. Miss Jade is safe and on her way home. Go to your door. She'll be there any minute." The bird flew away.

Brittany bolted from the bedroom. She heard Rose laughing as she unlocked the door. As soon as the door opened, Brittany slipped out and ran toward the basket.

"Well, well, so we finally meet," purred Blackie. "I've heard about you, but have only seen you from a distance."

Blackie had taken Brittany by surprise. But he didn't frighten her. His deep voice was warm and friendly. She allowed him to approach her. They circled and sniffed one another.

"Come on, Blackie," called the porter.

"I have to go," Blackie said to the tabby kitten half his size. "What's it you're called? Ah yes, Britt the Kit. It suits you. My name is Blackie the Deli Cat." He sniffed the basket, "Jade, my love, see you soon." He trotted over to the elevator. Rose put Britt in the basket and went into the apartment.

CHAPTER FIVE

Rose let the basket fall from her arms onto the living room floor. As soon as she turned away, both cats popped out of the basket and ran into the bedroom.

Jade leaped on the bed and hissed, "Britt, no," stopping the kitten before she could jump on the bed. "Let me rest."

"No! Tell me what happened first. I was so worried. But you don't care about me. You care more about the little boy. Go on. Go to sleep. You never tell me anything! How did that black cat know my name, anyway?"

Jade laid down and moaned at Brittany's dramatics.

"The next time you try to get out, maybe Rose will catch you," Brittany whimpered.

"Okay, come up here." The kitten pounced on the bed.

"Start with Blackie the Deli Cat."

"He helped me get home. He lives downstairs in the delicatessen. I've known him since I was your age.

He's my consort. Do you understand what that means?" Jade asked.

"Does it mean if you weren't fixed you'd have his kittens?"

"Yes. That's one way of putting it."

"What about the boy? And who was that woman? I thought she was going to hit you."

"Tony and his mother were hugging when we left. Now will you let me rest?" Jade nudged her little sister.

"Sure." Brittany helped Jade bathe, then finally left her alone, snuggled and purring under the blanket covers.

After what seemed a short time Jade felt Brittany jump on the bed. "Jade, watch out!" the kitten called. But it was too late. Jade was being squashed. She let out a yelp and stuck her claws in whatever was on top of her.

"Ouch!" yelled Man. "Is that you, Jade? Sorry. I just sat down to take my shoes off. You didn't have to claw me." The cat began to purr. "Okay, so we're both sorry. Come on Britt, let the old girl sleep."

CHAPTER SIX

Jade slept through until dawn the next day. Brittany woke to her sister's purring. Jade was playfully trying to slip between Love's arms without waking her.

"Morning Jade," said the orange and white kitten as she stretched from head to tail.

"Hi. Come out on the terrace. These two won't be up for hours." Brittany let out a ferocious yawn, and followed Jade.

They settled next to one another in the early sunlight. Jade studied Britt for a moment. "I guess it's time I tell you about my city life, before we moved up here to a larger apartment, and you came to live with us. There was no Man back then, or a country home. Love and I lived in one room. She had to leave me during the day. You've always had me and known freedom. I was lonely and escaped to the streets to find friends."

"I'm glad Venice and Blackie are your friends. It's scary to imagine being alone, or never running free."

Brittany looked out on the city. "How come you stopped going out? Cause of me?"

"Yes and no. It's hard to get to the street from here, and I do have you and our country home. The one I miss is my Black." Jade sighed. Her green eyes squinted in the morning sun. "Maybe we can work something out. I'd like to take you out with us sometime. I'd introduce you to everyone as my Britt the Kit."

"That would be fantastic."

"Good," Jade said. "I'm hungry. Let's get them up for breakfast." The cats ran into the bedroom. They purred and pounced until Love and Man woke up.

During the next few weeks, Jade told Brittany about her city adventures. They watched from the window as Blackie and Tony became friends. The following week, Blackie succeeded in getting upstairs for a visit in the laundry basket. When Rose saw how the cats got along, she allowed him up whenever he was around.

One afternoon Venice landed on the terrace and called for the cats to come out.

"What is it?" Jade asked, as she and Brittany rushed out.

"Look! Look up the street," Venice bobbed up and down, pointing with his wing. "Tony's father is home and healthy."

"That's good news, Venice." Jade began to purr.

"Look Jade," said Britt, "Blackie's sitting on Tony's front steps. They all look so happy I can almost feel it."

"Don't you just love a happy ending?" cooed Venice.

"I sure do," replied Miss Jade.

"Me too," purred Britt the Kit.

The End Of This Sweet Tale

CHARCOAL'S STORY

CHAPTER ONE

"Jade! Jade! Where are you?" Brittany cried, running from the backyard, through the swinging cat door, into the kitchen of her country home. The orange and white tabby kitten searched room by room for her older sister. She ran to all of Jade's favorite sleeping places – under the porch table, in the soft chair by the fireplace, up in the loft where there was a skylight window, and in the back of a dark coat closet. Finally, when she ran down the hallway towards the bedrooms, she spotted a lump moving in the bed of the humans the two adopted cats lived with, Love and Man. The room was dark and cool. She heard purring from underneath the soft flannel sheets and blanket.

"Jade! Wake up!" Brittany pleaded. She jumped onto the bed and pounced on the lump with her front paws. "I don't know what to do. I need you to help me."

Slowly, the mature, grey, Russian Blue cat appeared. "What is the matter, Britt?"

"Come outside with me. Please," Brittany whimpered.

Jade's nose twitched at the smell of fear coming from Brittany. "Go on. I'll follow," she said tapping the kitten's tail.

"You're the best." Brittany jumped from the bed, and ran back through the house, and out the cat door.

When Jade reached the outdoors she stopped for a moment to take in the view and breathe in the early spring air. Her lungs expanded with the sweet smell of new life. Tiny green leaves filled the trees, and pink and white blossoms dressed up the dogwoods. Bright yellow forsythia and daffodils were in bloom. The birds were home from their winter trips south, and the animals were awake from their winter sleep. She looked north and scanned the woods that bordered the spacious yard. Her round green eyes moved west to the cornfield that lay behind the woodshed where Man was chopping wood and listening to music on his iPod. She looked south to a group of fruit trees and berry bushes that were filled with nests of birds and the homes of small animals. Tall evergreens stood in the east protecting the house and land from the sights and sounds of the road.

"Jade!" Brittany yelled from the far end of the house.

"I'm coming."

The two cats entered the cluster of evergreens. As they moved through the low, thick branches, Jade followed the pure white tip of Brittany's bushy ringtail. They came to a little clearing where several animals, young and old, gathered in a circle. There were rabbits, squirrels, skunks, and a stately old woodchuck. In the trees, birds were quietly perched on branches.

Brittany moved to a small ball of fur that rested on a bed of leaves. "Here, Jade," she whispered.

Jade approached a tiny animal, and very gently turned it over with her paw. "It's a kitten! Ah, Britt, its hurt bad – can't be more than a few months old. Go get Man!"

"Yes! I hoped you'd say that!" Brittany immediately ran toward the woodshed, meowing to Man as loudly as she could.

"Hello there, Britt the Kit, great day to be alive," the man greeted her, as he split a huge log with his axe. "Huh? What is it, girl?" He pulled out his ear buds and dropped his axe. "Do you need me? Is it Jade?" Britt shrieked, and leaped three feet in the air.

"Okay. Go on," he followed her to the tree line. "You want me to go in there?" The kitten looked up with pleading golden eyes. "Okay," he said shaking his head. He bent down on his hands and knees and crawled in after her.

Back at the clearing, Jade carefully cleaned the kitten's wounds with her tongue. The creatures watched with concern. The tiny tomcat's fur was a mixture of black and white patches with smears of blood on its head, back, and paws.

"Will it live?" whispered a rabbit.

"Charcoal's gone beyond being a bully," cawed a Crow.

"Imagine its pain..." said a mouse.

"Wasn't it nice of Brittany to help?" chirped a robin.

"Be still," snapped the woodchuck. "And he is a male not an 'it'."

The kitten whimpered and looked up at Jade. "You're safe now," she said. When he began to shiver, Jade encircled his body with hers to keep him warm. After he was snug and secure, she acknowledged the woodchuck.

"Hello, Nathanial."

"It was good of you to come, Miss Jade. I'm sad to say Charcoal the Cat has struck again."

"Don't you think it's time you do something about him? As an Elder how can you keep ignoring his acts of cruelty? Remember his attack on Brittany last summer? She almost lost her leg, Nathanial," Jade growled.

"You're right, he's gone too far this time. I will call for a 'Meeting of Elders'. I would like you and Brittany to attend."

"We'd be honored," Jade replied.

Just then the bushes rustled and Brittany reappeared. He's behind me, Jade. I think he thinks you're hurt."

The towering evergreen limbs began to sway. They heard branches snap as the man made his way into the clearing. The animals scattered and hid.

"Jade, you okay? Come here, girl," he said, reaching for the cat's paw. Jade pulled away and hissed in protest. Brittany meowed and drew his attention to the kitten.

"What happened to you?" he whispered, and stroked the kitten's head with his finger. The tiny ball of black and white fur moved and opened its eyes. They were pools of navy blue. "Poor thing," Man said, scooping the kitten up in his large hand. "Good work, girls. We'll take care of this little one." As soon as he left the clearing Nathanial reappeared.

"Nathanial," Jade asked, "does his family know about this?"

"No, Miss Jade. He's from the big farm two roads over. I'll send word. And I'll set the meeting for moonrise tomorrow, at the abandoned barn on the hill. By then you should be able to tell us if the kitten will survive." Nathanial lowered his head.

Jade sensed his concern. "Have hope Nathanial. He's young and strong. We should go." Jade and Britt slipped away.

CHAPTER TWO

Man brought the tiny kitten into the kitchen and placed it on a cool marble counter-top. He called to his wife. "Love, please bring me the first aid-kit."

Love entered the kitchen with a shoebox filled with medical supplies. "What happened?" she asked.

"Something tried to kill this kitten. Look at these welts."

Love checked the kitten's bottom determining it was male. "Where did you find him?"

"In the evergreens," he answered. "Brittany came to get me. Jade was there, too."

"He's a cute little fellow. How badly do you think he's hurt?" Love asked.

"Nothing is broken. But these bites and scratches look nasty. He'll need antibiotics. Will you clean him up while I call Jen at the Animal Hospital?"

"Sure," Love said. She reached for a sterile gauze pad, dampened it with warm water, and carefully began to clean the kitten's wounds. Man left the house with his cell phone, letting the screen door slam. The sudden noise made the kitten jump and cry.

"It's okay. You're safe," Love said, stroking his chin. "Look up here. Let me see your face." She lifted his head with her finger. "Aren't you handsome. And your eyes are beautiful. But so very sad." Her soft voice reassured the kitten and he settled back down.

Love looked up at her two cats patiently waiting on the ledge of a pass-through counter. "I'm very proud of you two." The cats began to purr. "You saved this kitten's life."

Man returned a minute later: "Jen said to bring him right over to the hospital. A moment later he left with the kitten.

Later that afternoon while the three felines rested, Brittany asked, "Jade, why did Charcoal do this?"

"It isn't a question of why, Britt. When a bully is cruel it means they want to cause pain. They enjoy it and don't think or care about the consequences. That makes them dangerous. It's the reason why this time Charcoal's going to be held responsible for what he did."

"I think I understand." Britt replied.

They watched the kitten drift in and out of sleep. He was dreaming about his family and his farm. He wished he was home, even though his Mama was going to punish him for disobeying her. Charcoal couldn't have grabbed him if he hadn't broken the rule of never leaving the barn alone. Now he was paying the price. He would listen from now on.

CHAPTER THREE

As the moon rose the following night, Jade and Brittany followed the path to the old barn. They stopped just outside. "You go up to the hayloft, Brittany, with the rest of your young friends."

"Why can't I stay with you Jade?" Brittany whined.

"Because, this is how an Elders' meeting is conducted. You're supposed to go up there and be still."

"But…"

"But nothing. You'd all ask too many questions. We could spend the night satisfying your curiosity alone," Jade answered. "Now go on." Brittany reluctantly walked away. Jade took a moment and looked up at the clear night sky, and focused on the first star she spotted and made this wish: "Star light, star bright, please, grant this tale a happy ending tonight."

Then, as Jade stepped inside the barn, she observed an extraordinary picture. Representing the area's farms and forests were a variety of animals, birds, and insects milling around peacefully.

"Hello, I'm Randy," whispered a voice next to Jade's ear. She turned to discover she was eye to eye with a dangling, rust-colored wolf spider.

"Hi, do you live here?" Jade calmly asked.

"Aren't you a cool one? Didn't I scare you?"

"No. Did you want to?"

"Maybe. If you give me a ride I'll show you around."

"Thanks, I'll find Nathanial. Bye." Jade gave the spider a tap with her paw, leaving it swinging on its own silky line.

"Miss Jade," Nathanial called, and then waved for her to join him in the center of the barn. "How is the kitten?"

"He'll be fine, Nathanial. And, I'd venture to say he'll be the best behaved kitten on his farm," Jade purred.

"That's wonderful. Everyone, please, let's begin." The woodchuck announced, and made circling motions with his paws to gather the creatures close to him. "Since I called this meeting, I will choose the number of Elders for tonight's inner circle."

"But first, I want to introduce two special guests. First, please meet the lovely cat at my side, Miss Jade, who has just reported that the injured kitten will make a complete recovery. Second, up in the hayloft, is her little sister, Brittany, known to us affectionately as 'Britt the Kit'."

Jade and Brittany each took a bow.

"All right, Nat let's begin," huffed a huge rabbit elder named Chief. "Choose your inner circle."

Several creatures raised their voices asking to be included. "Quiet," Nathanial ordered. "I call Henry, the Labrador Retriever from the injured kitten's farm. I call Carlos, the crow. And, I call Sass, the red fox."

"Good pick," said Chief. He stamped his hind foot on the wood floor, making the noise of a hammer banging. Then, wiggling his nose and tail, he chased everyone else from the center of the large barn. "Come to order," he shouted. Then, in a softer voice, "Let us pray to our Earth Mother for guidance."

Everyone lowered their heads and a hush came over the barn.

A moment later Nathanial cleared his throat and the meeting began. He took a few minutes to explain Charcoal the Cat's vicious history. The woodchuck finished by saying, "I want that cat banished!"

"Nat, you can't do that," Henry responded. "I've explained this to you a hundred times. If he was raised to be dependent on humans for food, he doesn't know how to survive on his own."

"Who cares if he survives?" squawked Carlos. "That good-for-nothing doesn't deserve any better."

"May I speak?" called a voice from the outer circle.

"Who are you?" called Chief. The animals turned to see a black tomcat enter the barn.

"I'm Jake, the victim's father."

"Yes, of course," Sass replied in a gentle voice.

"First, I want to thank Jade and Britt for saving my son. Second, I ask that Charcoal's punishment be painful and that he be scarred," demanded the father.

"Yes, of course you would want that," Sass agreed, her bushy red tail swaying as she circled and stopped in front of the cat. "You must leave his fate to us." Her amber eyes burned into his cold blue eyes. There was a long moment before the cat backed down. "Continue, Nathanial," said the fox.

"Thank you, Sass," said the woodchuck. "Now I would like to hear from Miss Jade."

As Jade looked around the barn she felt admiration for the deer, squirrels, birds, rabbits, and raccoons that all stood peacefully next to one another. "See how you all are here, respecting each other's right to exist, Charcoal has lost that part of himself. In New York City where I grew up, we separate reckless troublemakers from the community."

"Interesting," said Sass. "I like the way you think."

"Actually," said Henry, "we do it all the time on the farm. Certain undesirables are kept separate. And others, like the chickens, are protected. They have their own coop."

"And," Jade added, "after Charcoal attacked Brittany, I taught her to stay on her own land where she was safe."

"I see," said Nathanial. "If he can't live with us in peace, he'll have to leave, or we will keep him on his land!"

"Good idea," said Carlos.

"And," Sass added, "we'll let him choose which he prefers."

"Agreed, Nathanial, you're brilliant," said Chief. "Miss Jade, would you like the honor of relaying our judgment to Charcoal?"

"Yes, I would. Thank you," Jade purred with satisfaction.

"Good," said Nathanial. "All right, this meeting is over. Let Charcoal's punishment serve as an example to all."

"A question," called a buck from the back of the barn.

"No more questions," growled the rabbit.

"It's a good one. Worth asking," said the buck.

"Let him speak, Chief," snapped Nathanial.

"What happens if the cat won't change?" asked the buck.

"We'll let Jake have him," Sass said, and everyone cheered.

"Well done," proclaimed the rabbit. "Go home. Be well. Stay safe. And may your bellies be full and your dreams sweet."

A group gathered around Jade. Nathanial made the introductions. Up in the hayloft, Brittany was bursting with pride and accepting compliments on Jade's behalf.

Sass and Henry moved to a corner. Their minds had locked on the same thought. "Jade is perfect. She is wise and caring. We'll ask her to join us as an Elder."

CHAPTER FOUR

A few days later when the kitten was feeling better, Jade took him out to the backyard. His wounds were healing nicely. The medicine from the animal hospital prevented an infection, and he grew stronger on Love's chicken and warm milk. While they were resting on the thick green grass, enjoying the sun's warmth, Jade saw Brittany bolt from the woods and run into the house. Jade looked toward the woods and spotted a crow circling above the trees.

"It's Carlos," Jade whispered. "The crows were assigned to keep watch over Charcoal – the cat must be in the woods." She nudged the sleeping kitten, "Let's go into the house."

His sleepy blue eyes popped open. "Why?" he asked, as a big yawn escaped his little body. His mouth opened so wide he fell over backwards. "Can't we stay longer? The sun feels good."

"No! We can't!" Jade nudged him with her nose.

"Ouch. That hurt." He wouldn't budge.

"I don't have time for this. If you won't move on your own, I'll carry you." So she picked him up with her mouth by the back of his neck, and sprinted into the house. Placing him on the kitchen floor, she said, "Find Brittany, and stay with her."

"It's him, isn't it, Miss Jade?"

"Yes," Jade said softly. The kitten ran away whimpering.

Jade left the house, jumped onto a porch table, and became intensely alert. The pupils of her eyes narrowed to straight black slits. Her nose twitched as she sniffed the air. Her keen ears strained to pick up sounds. Her blue-grey fur stiffened, doubling in size. A moment later her green eyes locked on a pair of yellow eyes hidden among the forsythia bushes that bordered the woods. It was Charcoal.

"So the Queen is out and looking about," Charcoal called from the woods. "Looking for me, are we? Yes, it appears so," he growled. "Thought I'd be locked in for life, did we? No way. I got out. All the neighbors called to say what a bad 'Tom' I was. Mean old me... hurt a kitten. Shame, shame. The little brat was out of his barn. He was fair game... and sweet at that. And now, the brave Miss Jade, whose sister tells tales of your adventures in the streets of the great city, sits puffed and proud."

Jade jumped off the table and moved toward him across the lawn. "I knew your humans wouldn't keep you caged. Besides, it's not up to them to decide what's to be done with you."

"Done with me?!" said Charcoal, leaping from yellow flowers. "Never mind that. Let me look at you. My, you are a beauty. I never knew. I didn't..."

Jade moved quickly, ignoring his words. He cowered as she approached him. When she was upon him, inches from his face, she hissed and said with a hot breath, "How dare you harm a newborn? Are you sick?" She spit and scratched his face with an open claw, tearing the tender skin below his ear.

Charcoal crouched to the ground and hissed. "Is this a city way of greeting? Interesting? You've made your point. I didn't know you had such a temper. But you are no match for me."

"I have no desire to match you. I have a message for you from your Elders. A meeting was held to discuss your attack on the kitten. They decided to put an end to your acts of cruelty."

"What's that supposed to mean?' he snarled, digging his claws into the earth. "I wasn't told about a meeting!"

"Either you change your ways, Charcoal, or leave the area. But understand, if you choose to stay and bully or abuse anyone else, you will be confined to your land. You will lose your freedom."

He laughed. "No one can tell me how to live my life."

"Not true. You lost that right when you crossed the line of fairness as given by our Earth Mother. You've hunted to harm for sport, not food. You maimed for play, interested only in your own pleasure. Choose wisely, and know you are being watched." Jade started to back away.

"You're leaving? The 'choice' as you put it, stinks. And I've just begun with you, beauty."

He was about to attack when a stone hit him in the chest and knocked the wind out of him.

"Don't even think about it, Charcoal," Love yelled, ready with a bigger rock aimed at his head. "Get out of here. NOW!" Without hesitation, the cat disappeared into woods.

Jade ran to Love and allowed her to be picked up. "What were you doing?" the woman asked as she hugged her cat. "Avenging the kitten? Please Jade, stay away from that cat. Let his people be responsible for him."

"No, Love," Jade purred and relayed to the woman holding her in her arms. "We all need to be responsible for each other. I know you believe in that truth." Jade rubbed her head against Love's chin as she was carried home.

Charcoal watched them from the woods. "Very touching," he growled. "Round one goes to the good guys. We bad guys will have to be more careful from now on."

CHAPTER FIVE

Charcoal headed home through the woods. "Why do I feel so twisted inside? This is my domain." He muttered under his breath. "I can out-run, out-hunt, and out-maneuver everyone around here." A tree branch snapped behind him. "Who's there?" he hissed, spun around, eyes and ears alert, but saw nothing. Cautiously, he continued. "What am I so worried about? A city Queen, with a strong left hook, who rarely leaves her land?" Charcoal couldn't shake the feeling that he wasn't alone, "I know you're there. Show yourself. I demand it!"

Brittany stepped out of the shadows. "How'd ya like my big sister, Charcoal?" She ran past him so fast, all he saw was a flash of orange. All he felt was the wind she left behind.

Suddenly, four striking crows swooped down, and hit him on the back. Their claws left raw thin scratches. "Beware cat," called Carlos. "We've got you covered from above."

As Charcoal watched the birds fly away, the woods began to echo with the bark of dogs. He panicked when he saw Henry a few feet away. "You've gone too far, cat. How about I take you between my teeth and toss you about?" he snarled.

"Come on," Charcoal shouted. "You can't be serious. You can't mean this? The kitten is okay. It's over. I won't do it again." A shadow slowly moved over the charcoal-grey cat. He cowered to the ground. His ear pressed against his head, and the muscles in his neck tightened. The fur on his back rose, as he swung around to face whatever was behind him.

"Yes, it is over, Charcoal the Cat," challenged Nathanial. The woodchuck's image was backlit by the sun. "Miss Jade spoke for us all."

"I was just goin' home," the cat growled.

"Is that all?" Nathanial sneered. "Perhaps you didn't grasp the opportunity she presented. Let me make it, and my position, clear to you. If I had my way you'd be banished. And if you returned, you'd be killed. I have no patience for the human attachments you domestics need for survival. However, there are those who believe you must be given a chance, because you are dependent on people for food and shelter. So be smart and mend your ways." Nathanial stepped away. The sunlight glared into the cowering cat's eyes.

Charcoal stepped behind a tree branch to shield himself from the sun's light. "Gee Nat, I'm sorry you feel that way," he said sarcastically. "Can I go now, oh great one?"

"Don't be a wise guy Charcoal," said Sequanku the skunk. His black and white head popped out of a hole in the ground. "I'll fix it so your nose can't smell, but everyone will sure smell you."

"Shut up, stinker," Charcoal hissed. "You don't scare me." He turned in disgust, and moved somberly through the forest. The presence of other animals was overwhelming. "I can't believe this has gone so far."

"Hey, Charcoal!" yelled the injured kitten. He was standing on a large rock flanked by Jade and Brittany.

Charcoal saw the kitten and moaned. "Now what? You want to tell me how mean I was to hurt you? Why didn't you stay in the barn? None of this would be happening if you minded your Mama."

"Oh, really, Charcoal. You're going to blame this kitten for your troubles?" questioned Jade, almost amused.

"No, you've had your say. Let the little one speak."

"I want you to know I'm going to grow up thanks to everyone here," stated the kitten. "Jade is going to teach me to fight, and someday I'll be the strongest. So don't you ever hurt anyone again, 'cause when I'm grown, you won't even be safe on your land! You hear me?" the kitten screamed with every ounce of his tiny being.

"Sure, kid. We all need goals." He turned and disappeared in the thick undergrowth of the woods.

When Charcoal got home, a jingle bell collar was fastened on his neck. His mistress scolded him for sneaking out, and he was ordered down a flight of stairs to his dark damp basement.

"This has not been a good day," he moaned. He drank some water, and ate some food that had been left for him, and settled down on an old couch to bathe and sleep.

"They've cornered me," he said puzzled. "Why?" He ripped at the couch with his claws, and bit hard on an old velvet pillow. Restlessly, he paced the basement, jumped around knocked things over, and made a terrible racket. Nothing eased his misery. He even tried to claw his way out of a window, but the metal screen only snapped his claws and caused his paws to bleed.

Eventually he returned to the couch and drifted into a nightmarish sleep. Uncontrollable visions and voices ran through his mind. He heard the kitten yelling, "I'll be bigger and stronger..." the skunk teasing, the dog snapping at his tail... but worst of all was a black shadow that was chasing him. Charcoal couldn't get away or hide. Everywhere he turned the shadow was there. He tried swiping at it with an open claw, but found no flesh. When it spoke, the voice was deep and profound. "You weren't always bad," it kept repeating. "Find the good. Look for it – here, inside you. Do it now – before you're caged, confined as a house cat. You will lose your precious freedom."

Charcoal screamed himself awake. He panted and threw himself about in a rage. "Why are they after me? I like the way I am. I have fun. I'm a cat. But I can't be caged. I'll obey. Do as they say. For now..." he whispered. Then he used his rough tongue to smooth his fur, and calm himself. He was afraid to sleep, too afraid he'd dream again.

CHAPTER SIX

That same night a celebration was taking place at Jade and Brittany's home. The kitten was going back to his family at the farm. The three cats sat happily on the dining room table. Love and Man stood near.

"It's time to go, little one," Love said, bending over and kissing the top of the kitten's head. He'd found a place in her heart. "From now on you listen to your Mama. We'll visit you next weekend." The kitten jumped into her arms and licked her face. "We have a surprise for you. Anna, the farmer's wife, asked us to name you, in honor of having saved your life."

"We know how important a cat's name is," Man proudly added.

"Jade, Britt, we hope you agree with our decision."

The two cats exchanged a curious look. The kitten sat proud and anxious between his two friends.

"I've decided, and my husband agrees, that your name shall be 'Sky', and here are the reasons why. Your fur holds the light of day and the dark of night. Your eyes change color with your mood, much like the sky changes with the weather and seasons. When you were hurt, they were a deep dark stormy blue. Today when you returned from the woods, they were a strong light blue with yellow specs of sunshine."

Man scooped the kitten up and held him over his head, "We name you Sky! We hope you have a long life filled with many daughters and sons. Jade. Brittany. Meet Sky." He put the kitten back down on the table. Sky pranced around purring proudly. Jade and Brittany meowed their approval.

"It's gonna be quiet around here without Sky," said Britt.

"Yes. Sky is fun," Jade agreed. "But I like our family just the way it is." Jade moved close to Brittany and rubbed against her. "Did you know Nathanial asked me to be an Elder?"

"That's great!" said Britt the Kit. "It looks like this tale has a happy ending."

"I'd say so. Sky is going home good as new. Charcoal is not going to be allowed to hurt anybody anymore. Yes," Jade purred. "It's a happy ending."

The End Of This Sweet Tale

HARRY'S STORY

CHAPTER ONE

It was a perfect day. The air was filled with extra oxygen, the sky was an extra blue, and the grass was extra green. The birds were flying higher, and singing their sweetest tunes. Bugs darted to and fro, riding the breeze, soaring like spaceships. All the animals were light on their feet, looking for fun and someone to share the warm sunny day with.

Jade and Brittany were out on their land visiting Nathanial the woodchuck. The cats discovered him working in the woodshed, which was also his home.

A voice called out from the vegetable garden: "Brittany! You wanna go across the road and run?" It was Boots, an adorable two-year-old rabbit who lived in a warren near by. Boots was Brittany's favorite playmate. His youthful body was covered with soft tan fur. He had brown and white specks on his back, a snowball tail, and four pure white paws.

"Definitely," Britt answered. "But we have to get back before dark. I got yelled at when I got home last time; Love was worried," complained the orange and white tabby kitten.

"Crossing the road after dark," cautioned her older sister Jade, "is a good way to end up as road-kill."

"Yes, children," added Nathanial, "the road is very unpredictable."

"Don't worry. I'll watch out for Brittany," Boots said, thumping his hind paw.

"Brittany," Jade said, "while you're over there, check on Harry for me. He seems troubled."

The elders watched as the two youngsters ran off to play across the road.

"Be careful," Jade called after them. "What a pair."

"That they are, Miss Jade," added Nathanial. "It fascinated me to watch them become friends. A cat and rabbit are such an unlikely pair."

Britt and Boots reached the wide blacktop road. One looked to the left; the other looked to the right. When they both yelled "all clear" at the same time, they raced across.

"You always win," huffed Brittany.

"I'm a rabbit. We're the fastest," Boots responded proudly. "Let's go for a run before we visit the old stallion."

"Why'd you say stallion? Harry's a horse."

"I know but he's a male horse and they're called stallions and female horses are called mares."

"I didn't know that. Does everyone have special boy-girl names?" asked Brittany.

"Yeah, I think so. Rabbits do. I'm a buck and my sister, Popup, is a doe. Don't you know what they are for cats?"

"No." The kitten's bushy ringed tail swished back and forth.

"Don't be upset," said Boots. "Ask Miss Jade. I don't know a lot of stuff either."

"Not knowing," Brittany complained, "makes me feel dumb."

"We're not dumb, we're young. My Dad calls it inexperience. Come on, let's play."

Harry, the palomino stallion, spotted Brittany and Boots as they ran through his open meadow. He watched them take turns chasing one another around the great weeping willow trees. He laughed as they played a jumping game, which took them back and forth across the stream on his land.

When Brittany and Boots tired they rested by the stream, and treated themselves to a cool drink of water. "I really needed that run, Boots," said Brittany. I'm happy we're gonna be here with Love and Man for summer vacation."

"You live with nice humans. They never scare me." Boots sat up and wiggled his nose, sniffing the air. "We'd better go visit Harry now, or you won't get home before dark."

They found Harry in his corral.

"He's a mess," said Boots.

"Look, his beautiful white mane and tail are all knotted." Brittany whispered.

As they approached the large tan-colored animal, Boots called out: "Hi, Harry. What happened to you?"

"Yeah, Harry," added Brittany, "you don't look so good."

"I know, but the two of you look wonderful. I watched you play. Britt the Kit, you've become quite a runner," Harry said.

"Thanks," she said, jumping onto the wooden fence.

Boots hopped closer and rested his front paws on the bottom of the corral. "So Harry, what's up with you? Miss Jade sent us to check on you."

"I'm doing fine, Boots. It's just that my folks have been too busy to groom me, and they're low on money for my feed. I'm expensive, you know." He shook his head and let out a loud snort, "I may be going to Luther's."

"Oh no, not Luther's!" the rabbit gasped.

"What's Luther's?" asked Brittany.

"We don't really know, Britt. No one has ever come back from there," Boots whispered.

"That's scary. You don't want to go, do you Harry?" asked Brittany.

"Of course I don't, Britt. This is the only home I've ever known. It'll mean leaving my family and friends. I'll be alone, nothing will be familiar, and everything will be strange. I love every inch of my land, and I have no idea what will happen to me if they send me away."

"Okay, take it easy." Brittany jumped from the fence, suddenly uncomfortable with the horse's size. "We'll tell Jade. She'll know what to do. She's real smart, Harry. Come on Boots."

The horse watched the tiny cat and rabbit until they were safe on the other side of the road.

CHAPTER TWO

Brittany slipped through the swinging cat door. The house felt empty. She gobbled down a plate of cat food, took a long slow drink of water, and settled on her chair in the living room. She stretched from head to tail and began to bathe. She washed her paws and face, and before long fell asleep to the sound of her own purring.

A few hours later Jade came into the room and jumped onto the same chair. The older Russian Blue cat sniffed her adopted sister's fur, picking up the scents of the different places Brittany had been. The sleeping tabby smelled of the field, stream, and Harry's coral. Jade stopped when she smelled the horse. "Britt the Kit," she called the kitten softly from sleep. "Wake up. What happened with Harry?"

Brittany stretched and yawned. "You were right. He's got trouble." She looked up at her sister with questioning golden eyes. "Jade, what are the boy and girl names for cats?"

"Tell me what Harry said before you start asking a lot of questions."

"No. You tell me. Boots knows what he is," Britt protested.

"All right. Male cats are called 'Tom' and we're called 'Queen'," Jade answered with pride.

"Queen! That's the best." Brittany purred.

"It is, isn't it? Now, get back to the horse."

"You mean stallion. That's what a male horse is called."

"You're making me angry. Do you want to feel my claws?"

"Harry's unhappy because he may be going to Luther's."

"Last-chance Luther's... Oh no," Jade sighed. "That's too bad." Jade curled up sadly on a pillow next to her sister.

"Why'd you call it 'Last-chance' Luther's, Jade?"

"It's what Cora Sue called it. She's a carriage horse, I mean mare, a friend, from Central Park in the city."

"Jade..."

"What?"

"I kinda told Harry you'd help him."

Jade's round green eyes opened wide. "You did! How can I possibly help him, Brittany?"

"If anyone can, you can. Tell me about Cora Sue." Brittany snuggled close to Jade.

The two cats lay nose to nose as Jade remembered...

It was Jade's first overnight trip with Blackie the Deli Cat. He had taken her to Central Park, a wonderful place in New York City. Late in the evening they met a chestnut mare named Cora Sue. The horse was attached to a red carriage with colorful fresh flowers and ribbons all over it. Her driver took customers for rides around the park and city too. There was much to see in the park: a zoo, a carousel, ponds and lakes, 'Strawberry Fields', and statues of famous people, characters from books like 'Alice In Wonderland', and animals, too. Cora Sue told them that hers was an important job. She was a proud southern belle, born on a farm in Virginia...

"I had a wonderful life," Cora Sue had told her. "I was ridden for enjoyment and fed the best oats. When I grew older, I was put out to pasture to share my wisdom with the younger horses, and watch the clouds and seasons roll by. Then, one day, I was loaded onto a trailer with several other horses and taken from my home. I wound up at Luther's, 'Last-chance' Luther's. It's an evil place, children." Cora Sue neighed and shook her head. "The smell of fear was everywhere. Men dragged us from the trailer, and whipped us until we were locked in a large corral. An unfamiliar stallion approached me. He told me I would be going up for auction, and if I wasn't purchased that night I would never leave Luther's. I can still hear his words: 'Look and prance your prettiest, dear lady. Your life depends on it.'

"Then, a group of men entered the corral and began to look us over. I caught the attention of a kind-looking, gray-haired man, and turned on my southern charm. 'Aren't you a friendly one?' he said, as he checked my legs and teeth. 'You're healthy too. For a fair price I'll take you with me to the Big Apple.'"

Cora Sue thought he was talking about real apples, her favorite treat. She put her head on his shoulder.

"She was lucky," Jade said. "He took her out of there."

"Wow!" Britt exclaimed. "They don't have places like that for cats, do they, Jade?"

"No Brit. Not like that. Evidently, cats don't taste good. Sorry I scared you, but you wanted to know why Cora Sue called it 'Last-chance' Luther's."

When Brittany had fallen back to sleep, Jade moved to a cozy window seat. She looked up at the twinkling stars and mystical crescent moon that hung low in the clear summer sky. The night was as perfect as the day. A cool breeze drifted through the window carrying the sweet night air.

"Wishing to the crescent moon and stars, Miss Jade?" asked Nathanial. "I just treated myself to a delicious dinner from your veggie garden."

"I hope you left some for my family, Nathanial."

"Of course I did." He lowered his head. "I'm a woodchuck, not a pig."

"Sorry," Jade responded. "Britt has given me a tough problem to solve concerning Harry."

"What is the problem, Miss Jade?"

"Harry may be going to Luther's." The woodchuck frowned. "Luther's is a bad place, Nathanial. Could you help me? I need to know everything about Harry if we're going to save him."

"Of course," the woodchuck said, climbing onto a low tree branch near Jade's window.

They spent the night talking and planning. It was almost dawn when Jade left home and followed Nathanial across the road. They found Harry outside his barn moping around the corral.

"Harry," Nathanial called. "Look who I've brought for a visit." Jade leaped onto the corral, and approached the horse.

"Hello, Miss Jade," Harry said softly. "Nat shouldn't have brought you here. I know you can't help me. No one can."

"That's not true. Listen to her, please," urged Nathanial.

"Harry," Jade said, "let me tell you the story of a friend who went through Luther's. Please keep in mind that I met her after she'd been there." Harry listened patiently to Cora Sue's story.

"That's a nice story, but it doesn't help me. I'm doomed."

"No you're not," snapped Nathanial, "and don't start feeling sorry for yourself."

"Harry," Jade interrupted, "we can't stop them from sending you away, but there should be time to give you a chance at a new life. Maybe even with the gray-haired man if you're lucky. Nathanial told me that you're smart and well trained. Is that true?"

"Yes. I was a dashing thoroughbred in my day, but that was a long time ago."

"That's right," said Nathanial, "and when I told Jade how lazy you've gotten, because your humans neglected you..."

"I realized," Jade interrupted, "that we can help you. We'll get you fit and trim, Harry. Starting tomorrow we're going to send Britt and Boots over here to work you out. When we're finished," Jade stroked Harry's nose with her paw, "you'll be in the best shape of your life."

"You're both pretty wonderful, and I'm touched. But..."

"...No 'buts' about it, Harry." Nathanial stated without any doubts. "You just do it! Give yourself this chance."

"I'll give it a try," Harry said half-heartedly. "Thanks Miss Jade. You too, old friend, and now please escort this fine lady home."

"Harry, before I go," Jade asked sincerely, "would you do something for me?"

"Certainly, Miss Jade."

"If you do have to go, and when you are settled in your new home, please send word. Give this tale a happy ending."

"I will. And thank you both for having so much faith in me." With that said, Harry bowed to the Russian Blue Queen. The stallion watched as the cat and woodchuck made their way back across the road. As the sun rose over Harry's meadow, he felt its warmth and he felt hope as his spirit stirred deep within him.

CHAPTER THREE

The following week was a busy time for everyone, especially Harry. Each morning, when his family left for work, Brittany and Boots crossed the road and went straight to his corral.

Following Nathanial's instructions, Brittany jumped onto the top post that held the latch that kept Harry locked in as Boots stood below her. When the cat was in position, the rabbit would jump and knock the latch into the air. As he did this, Brittany would push the gate open with her front paws. Harry then finished the job by giving the gate a push with his nose and running out into his field.

"Come on, Harry," called Britt. "It's time to do your stuff." Each morning they took turns running with the stallion. Their job was to get Harry in shape… fit and trim.

"Let's play chase, Harry," Boots yelled. The horse chased the rabbit all over. Boots got Harry to make sharp turns around the trees to strengthen his legs. Britt made him jump back and forth across the stream with her. The three finished up by running across the open meadow as fast as they could. It was a good workout. All the while, they cheered Harry on and, when he got tired, they encouraged him to keep going.

After only a week they saw a change in Harry. His legs were steadier when he circled the trees. He didn't breathe as hard, or overheat as quickly. His thick tan coat began to shine. His long white mane and tail trailed in the wind when he ran with Britt and Boots.

Late one night, Harry's mistress came into the barn to groom him. She brushed his body, and combed and braided his tail. "I'm sorry I've had so little time for you lately, Harry. I've been working at the mall, a double shift, to make enough money to keep you," she said softly in his ear as she combed his mane. "Harry, you are my best pal. We just can't afford you anymore. Next month, we have to take you to Luther's." The woman threw her arms around Harry's neck and began to sob.

When his mistress left the barn, he followed her out and watched her until she closed the door to the house. Restlessly, he circled the corral. He whinnied and cried and kicked out in frustration. "Why! Why do I have to leave? I belong here." His hooves pounded the dirt, and he circled faster and faster.

A voice came from out of the shadows. "Calm down." It was Nathanial. "What's got you so troubled, Harry?"

"It's definite, Nat. I'm leaving. I'll be gone before the moon is full. I'll never see you again. I'll never have a home here again."

"I'm so sorry. I will miss you, Harry." Nathanial sighed, resigned to Harry's fate.

"I remember when I got here; you stayed with me all night for weeks, right there in the barn, because I was scared. Well, I'm scared now too. What's gonna happen to me, Nat?"

The woodchuck moaned softly to himself. He wanted to be strong for Harry's sake.

"Listen to me. I have always been truthful with you, haven't I?" Harry nodded. "You look wonderful. Working with Brittany and Boots has brought you back to life. Jade's plan has worked. Harry, you know that don't you?"

"Sure. But…" his voice trailed off.

"No. Forget the 'buts'. You go and make a new life for yourself. And Harry…"

"Yeah, Nat."

"Every time I look over here I'm going to picture the way your head goes up and down when you're really happy and full of laughter. And I'll smile every time, I promise."

"I'll never find another friend like you, Nathanial."

"You won't have to Harry. I'll always be in your heart."

CHAPTER FOUR

"Jade! Come quick! Harry's leaving." Brittany was in a panic.

"Go get Nathanial", Jade said calmly. "He'll want to say goodbye." Jade jumped out on to the lawn from an open window. She ran to where she could see across the road. A moment later she was joined by Nathanial and Brittany. They watched the activity in Harry's corral. The stallion was kicking and rearing up – fighting hard to stay out of the trailer. He was not making it easy for his people.

"He's breaking my heart," said Nathanial, "Miss Jade, he's so frightened. I wish I could help him."

"Go over there," Jade said. "His humans won't pay any attention to you, they're too busy."

"I'll go with you, Nathanial," said Brittany. "Someone's got to calm Harry down before he has a heart attack."

When they reached the corral, Britt ran through the fence, meowing as loud as she could, and then circled back to Nathanial. Harry spotted them and Jade across the road.

"Calm down, old friend. Fighting won't help," said Nathanial. "Look for the gray-haired man. Remember what Jade said. Please Harry, go peacefully."

Harry heard his friend and yielded. His time to leave had come. He looked out to his field, filled his lungs with the sweet air of his home and soared high, reared up one last time and said, "Goodbye. Remember me. I'll remember you. Thanks, Miss Jade." He landed hard. His hooves pounded the ground.

Sensing his resolve, his mistress motioned for everyone to back away from her horse. Harry turned to Nathanial. "You are my true friend, Nat. Be well. Britt the Kit, my thanks to you and Boots, when you run my meadow, think of me."

Harry trotted over to his mistress, who had groomed him and braided his mane and tail with blue satin ribbons. He placed his head on her shoulder. They had shared a love. The pain of parting filled both their hearts. She held him tightly, and began to cry softly. "Good luck Harry," she whispered and released him with a gentle push.

Proudly, the stallion gave one long last look around, and allowed himself to be loaded into his trailer.

CHAPTER FIVE

Later that night Harry was led from the same corral Cora Sue had told Jade about. He was taken with several other horses into a large arena. It was very noisy. There were more people inside than Harry had ever seen in his life. They were yelling and whistling from seats high above him. The horses were poked and prodded by cowboys as they stood in line waiting to enter an enormous ring.

A man on a high stage spoke so loudly that Harry's ears pressed against the side of his head. Several horses, frightened by the voice, broke from the line. They jumped and whinnied. One poor stallion bolted and ran from the arena. Harry remained still and kept himself composed. He knew this was the hour he and his friends had worked so hard for. His last chance was at hand.

When Harry got to the head of the line he was hit hard on the rump and sent into the ring. He did his best to tune out the thundering noise of the spectators. He stopped and shook his head. "It's time. I've done the work. I'm ready to take my chance." Harry then focused on Nathanial's words and Jade's faith. A moment later he was ready. He raised his head and tail, determined to travel the ring and prance his way to victory.

As Harry neared the far end of the arena he spotted a gray-haired man studying his movements. He saw approval in the man's steel-blue eyes. Harry felt proud, and quickened his stride. He thought about running in his field with Britt and Boots. The second time around Harry became brazen. When he saw the same man watching, Harry turned and winked. The gray-haired man laughed in acknowledgement, and gave Harry a 'thumbs up'.

Harry whinnied and took one more turn around the arena. This time he had fun. He moved past the other horses with a light heart and a dance in his hooves. Harry felt sure he'd won his chance at a new home and life.

CHAPTER SIX

Several weeks later, as a new day was dawning, Brittany watched the sky from the terrace of their New York City apartment. One by one she saw the last few stars disappear and give way to the morning sunlight. She rolled onto her back and let out a huge yawn.

"Top of the morning, Britt the Kit!" called Blackie the Deli Cat. He was across the street, on the roof of a tenement building. Brittany was startled and fell off the chair.

"Sorry Britt," Blackie said, "I didn't mean to scare you."

"You didn't scare me," Brittany answered immediately. "How come you're over there? Are you always up this early?"

"I haven't been to sleep yet, just getting home. I need to have a word with Jade. Be a sweet kit and go get her for me."

"Can't. She's asleep. Come back later."

"Can't. I have to see her now."

"She'll hurt me, Blackie."

"No she won't. Just purr in her ear that it's about Harry."

"Harry! Don't move! We'll be right back!" Brittany ran into the apartment.

She found Jade sleeping, snuggled in their mistress Love's arms. For a moment she watched with envy, then cautiously approached the bed, stood on her hind legs, and gently touched Jade's nose with her paw. The peacefully sleeping cat stirred slightly and growled a warning. The kitten cringed, but did it again. This time Jade's eyes opened, giving Brittany a piercing icy green stare. "It's Blackie. It's important. Hurry!" she whispered. "It's about Harry."

"Blackie? Harry?" Jade yawned. In an instant she was wide-awake and slipped out of the sleeping woman's arms.

When Jade came out on the terrace, she found Brittany walking along the rail, and flirting with Blackie. "Really," Brittany purred, "you think I'm adorable, too. Well, I think you are very handsome."

"He's mine, brat," Jade growled playfully. "Get down, before you fall or I push you... Where's 'my' Blackie?"

Brittany jumped down and rubbed against her sister. "He's over there Jade, see?"

"Morning, Jade," Blackie called. "Were you dreaming about me?"

"Always. Please tell me about Harry!"

"You've done it again. I'm proud of you, my Pussy Willow. I was just telling Brittany that her hard work paid off. Cora Sue told me the whole story last night."

"Jade," purred Britt, "Harry found the gray-haired man."

"Blackie," said Jade, "you couldn't have brought me better news. Did you see him?"

"No, just Cora Sue. Luckily they wound up in the same stable. She said she's falling in love."

"Really." Jade purred. "How about Harry?"

"She said he's quite smitten. When he learns to pull a carriage and starts to work in the park, I said I'd bring you for a visit."

"Me too?" Brittany cried.

"It will be my pleasure to take you both. Now it's time for me to sleep." Blackie left the roof, making his way down an old fire escape, and disappearing into the back door of the delicatessen.

"Jade, you did it!" said Brittany. "Harry's safe, and he's here, near us."

"I can't wait to tell Nathanial. He's been so sad since Harry left."

"Yeah, and you and Blackie are gonna take me to Central Park. Isn't life wonderful?" purred Brittany.

"It sure is," Jade purred with relief. "Especially now, that this tale has a happy ending. The sun's up. Let's get Man up - it's time for our breakfast."

The End Of This Sweet Tale

THE PRINCE OF TAILS

CHAPTER ONE

"Hey, kit, over here," called a friendly voice from the snow-filled pine trees.

"Who is that?" asked Brittany. The young, orange and white, tabby kitten sat warming her paws on the only rock she could find that was free of snow and full of sun.

"Are you Britt the Kit?"

"Yes."

"Come into the wood," said the voice.

"No. You come out. The snow hurts my paws."

"The snow is wonderful. It shouldn't hurt."

"Who are you? I feel silly talking to someone I can't see."

"Here I am."

Brittany looked behind her and found she was face to face with a handsome red fox that was three times her size. A low whimper escaped her throat.

"Don't be frightened. I was looking for you."

"For me?"

"Yes. I need to speak with you. May I?" The fox tilted his head and studied her with piercing amber eyes.

"Can I ask a question first?"

"Go ahead."

"Are you a red fox?"

"Maybe." His eyes twinkled.

"Are you really a fox?" Brittany stretched her neck and gave him a sniff.

"Yes," he laughed. "And I am known throughout the county as the Prince of Tails. I have come to ask for your help, and that of your sister, Miss Jade."

"How could we help you?"

"I believe this forest and everyone who lives here is in danger. If you would both meet me and Nathanial the woodchuck here at dawn tomorrow, I'll explain the situation."

"I guess we could."

"Good. I must go now." A moment later the Prince of Tails disappeared into the thick woods.

"I can't believe it. I met a fox. I lived to tell the tale!" Brittany leapt from the rock and ran home.

When Brittany reached home she was happy to see the snow had melted and disappeared from her backyard. "Thanks, Sun," she said, facing west to see the setting sun. She slipped through their swinging cat door and entered her country home.

Brittany found her older sister, Jade, sleeping on a soft chair in front of the lit fireplace. I better not wake her, Brittany decided, as she smelled the Russian Blue cat's hot blue-gray silky fur. She settled on the floor nearby.

"Why so serious, Britt?" Jade asked a few minutes later when she stretched and turned to face the fire.

"I met a fox today. He's called the Prince of Tails," Brittany said as she stared into the flames.

"That's nice," Jade said, choosing to ignore what she thought was her adopted sister's imagination. "I wish you could see how beautiful you look, Britt. Your fur and the fire are the same burnt orange color. You could be the flame."

"You should see the Prince, Jade. He's amazing!" Brittany pulled her golden eyes from the fire. "He has a big black nose. His eyes, ears, and mouth are lined with black fur. And the entire underside of his body is snow white. He has long black-stocking legs with extra long black claws. The rest of him is a fiery fox-red. And his tail, Jade, his tail is bushy and bigger than me!"

Jade extended her head and sniffed Brittany's fur. "You did see a fox! Did he try to hurt you?"

"No. He was looking for me."

"Why?" hissed Jade.

"It's okay. I liked him. You will too. He wants us to meet him tomorrow, and Nathanial will be there too."

"To meet a fox and see Nathanial. I'll go." This should be interesting, thought Jade.

"Where are Love and Man? I'm hungry."

"Our darling humans went out for goodies. I heard them say it was going to snow again and we'd all tuck in for the night with good food, soft music, and a hot fire."

"Why is it still snowing? It's supposed to be spring."

"Earth Mother is just giving us a last taste of winter. Don't let it upset you. It won't last. I bet it's all gone by tomorrow. I heard Man tell Love he's going to play golf in the afternoon."

Both cats gave a quick turn when they heard their cat door snap closed. "Who's there?" Jade hissed a warning. Immediately they stood - their fur puffed doubling their size.

"It's me, Jerry. Is it safe to come in?" A tiny chipmunk stood timidly in the doorway of the living room.

"Yeah, we're over here by the fireplace," Brittany called.

"Hi," was all he could say as he stood in front of the fire and looked up at the two towering cats.

Jade noticed his fear and softly said, "It was very brave of you to come into our home uninvited, Jerry."

"Thanks, Miss Jade. I don't feel very brave. But I'm on assignment for the Prince. We changed the location of the morning meeting to your woodshed out back."

"How did you get invited?" Brittany growled.

"Don't be a brat, Britt. What's this about, Jerry?"

"All I know, Miss Jade, is that it has to do with the land. It must be bad, because when I got home the Prince was there. My Mama was crying and my Dad was screaming. I was sent here." They heard a truck door slam outside. "I gotta get out of here! You'll come, right?"

"Yes," was all Jade had time to say before the chipmunk took off, and dove headfirst out the swinging cat door, leaving the two cats very amused. "Come on, Britt, let's greet the folks."

"I hope they got shrimp!" said Brittany.

"I hope Love cooks a chicken," purred Jade.

CHAPTER TWO

"This is wrong!" Nathanial stated. The old woodchuck was a revered Elder among the animals. "The land was promised. Protected legally, by the man who built your home, Miss Jade. How can the humans break this promise, Tail?"

The fox's attention, at the moment, was focused solely on Jade, as hers was on him.

"Tail! What is the matter with you? Answer my question."

Brittany had been watching Jade and the Prince. She moved between the cat and fox to block their line of vision.

"I told you, Nat," said the fox. "There is a Land Developer who is trying to get a Variance." He spoke in a low deliberate voice. His tail swished back and forth.

"What is a Variance?" asked Jerry the chipmunk.

"Good question," said the Prince. "It is a legal paper people can apply for when – well, as Nat put it, they want to break a promise about land. In this case, a Land

Developer wants one so he can build new houses on top of your home, Jerry. We have to stop him in order to save the forest."

"How can I help you, Prince of Tails?" asked Jade.

"There are bright pink markers tied around the trees in the woods. If you can get your Man to see them, I believe he will stop the Developer for us."

"Why would he do that?" asked Brittany.

"Because," said the Prince, "he won't want any more building around here. There is a fair balance now, between the land, the humans, and us. The environment should stay protected."

"Furthermore, humans should keep their promises," added Nathanial.

"What else can we do?" asked the chipmunk.

"Keep this between us. If news gets out, everyone in the forest will panic and start to leave," said the fox.

"Uh, oh," said Jerry. "I wonder if my folks told anyone."

"Run quickly," ordered Nathanial. "Tell them to hold their tongues." The chipmunk was gone in a flash.

"Why would everyone leave?" Brittany was very confused.

"Because," Jade answered, "not all humans care about the lives of animals the way Love and Man do. Speaking of them, the sun is up. We'd better go before they spot us all together. I'll make sure they see the markers today."

"Thank you, Miss Jade. It was a pleasure to meet you," the Prince said as he bowed, "I'll be in touch." He turned to the woodchuck. "Nathanial, will you keep peace in the woods?"

"Yes, Tail," he replied. The Prince winked at Brittany and disappeared into the woods.

"Isn't he great, Jade?" mused Brittany.

"Yes, he is. Nathanial, how long have you known him?"

"I've known Tail since he was a pup, Miss Jade. He keeps an eye on the humans for us. He learned about their ways and laws by following them around the golf course where he lives, and eavesdropping on their conversations. He protects our interests and our lives."

Jade noticed a distant look in Nathanial's eyes.

"How did he come to take on such an important job?"

"It is not my story to tell, Miss Jade. All I will say is his first lessons from the humans were painful ones."

"I see. We better go, Nathanial. Will you be alright?"

"Yes. I must go too. But first, I want you both to know how pleased I am our Earth Mother placed you here with us."

"Thank you," Jade said and started home.

Brittany stayed behind, "Yeah, thanks Nathanial…"

The woodchuck could see a thousand questions in the young cat's eyes. He raised his paw to stop her.

"Not now, little one." Brittany turned and followed after Jade.

"Ah yes, dear Earth Mother," Nathanial sighed, "please watch over us all as we begin this quest to save lives and homes." Then the old woodchuck ambled into the woods.

CHAPTER THREE

"How are we gonna get Love and Man into the woods, Jade?" asked Brittany, after she devoured a bowl of food.

"It'll be easy. It's a beautiful day. The snow is gone. Spring is in the air. Love will go outside."

"You're right and Man will work in the garden."

"Find me when she leaves the house."

"What if you're sleeping? Can I wake you?"

"Yes. Just for today, I'll give you permission to wake me."

"Then what are you going to do?"

"When Love goes out, I'll go too. When she walks near the woods, I'll run in."

"But you don't like the woods." Brittany was surprised.

"I know, but she'll be curious and follow me."

"What about the pink markers and Man?"

"Love will take care of that part."

"Jade you're brilliant! What do we do now?"

"I'll nap on a sunny window sill. You go out and play."

Jade's plan did work easily. As soon as Love saw the bright pink markers tied around several trees she yelled for her husband to come into the woods.

"What is it, Love?" he said, as he joined her.

"What are those?" she asked pointing to the markers.

"Property markers. I wonder why they're here?"

"Me too? How can we find out?"

"When you drive me to the golf course this afternoon, ask George. He usually knows what's going on around here."

"Good idea," said Love. Brittany meowed as if to agree and led them out of the woods.

"Nice work, Miss Jade," said the Prince of Tails from behind a tree.

"It would be wise, dear Prince, not to sneak up on me. It could get you clawed," Jade hissed playfully.

"Since I always want to be wise," he appeared and grinned, "I won't do it again. I'd like it if you'd call me Tail."

"All right, Tail," Jade now purred, "If you drop the Miss."

"That's a deal."

"You sound like Man. He's a lawyer."

"I know. I follow him all the time around the golf course. We're both charming, too."

"I can see that. I have to go now. I hope we meet again."

"We will. Thanks for your help." The two parted.

George, the old caretaker of the golf course, was sitting on a lawn chair in front of the clubhouse. The big old house was also his home. "Afternoon Sir. And, you too pretty lady," he called to Love and Man as they got out of their truck.

"Hi, George!" called Love.

"See you later," her husband said. He waved to the old man.

"Isn't it a beautiful day?" Love asked, as she sat on the grass near George.

"No," he growled. "It's still too cold for these old bones to swing a golf club properly."

"Sorry to hear that. George, the woods near our house are filled with property markers. Do you know why?"

"No! Not again!" he got up and walked away.

"George, wait for me," she ran after him.

"Please stay here. I have to make a call." He went into the clubhouse. Love waited outside.

A few minutes later George walked out of the house. He looked as if someone had punched him in the stomach.

"What is it, George? You look awful," Love said.

"There's a Land Developer trying to buy up twenty acres of land. Some of it borders your property." George collapsed on a step.

"What are they going to do with it? It's all natural forest. And what about the animals?" She sat down next to him.

"The last time those guys built houses, hundreds of animals lost their lives and homes. Many of them moved here. Dear God, I don't want to watch that again."

"There are so many empty houses now, because of the economy, we certainly don't need any more around here!" Love's face turned the same pale color as George's.

"Can you and your husband help me fight this?"

"Definitely George, anything you want – you got it."

"Good. We'll have to move fast and gather support before the town council meets at the end of the month. This is a big election year. Those politicians won't be so quick to grant variances with a strong group of people against it."

Love understood and got up to leave. "I gotta go now. Will you call me?"

"Yes, as soon as I set things up." He reached out and took her hand. She helped him up.

"Try not to worry," Love said continuing to hold his hand.

"Me worry? Never. I'm gonna get mad. That is, as soon as I get this knot out of my stomach." George walked away rubbing his belly.

Later that night, George was waiting in the clubhouse, sitting in a large leather chair in front of an oversized fireplace. He gazed thoughtfully at the roaring flames while he waited patiently for his dinner guest, the Prince of Tails. The golf course was a long-time sanctuary for wild animals, because the game of golf requires several acres of protected land.

George sat up in his chair when he heard a thump on the porch. A gentle smile formed on his old wrinkled face. He looked around the side of his armchair. A soft 'yip' came from the handsome red fox framed in the window.

"Good evening to you, too. I had a feeling you'd show up tonight," George said. "I bet you had something to do with that pretty lady coming to see me today?" The fox yipped again. "I thought so. Come in, there's your dinner." George pointed to a bowl on the floor. The fox ran away. "Suit yourself. I'm in no mood to fuss with you." He sat back in the chair.

A few minutes later the Prince of Tails returned. The old man stood and faced him. "Tail, come in here. It's too cold for me out there." The fox didn't move. "I know about the land. We got a lawyer. This time we're gonna fight them." Tail leaped through the window and licked the old man's face.

CHAPTER FOUR

Jade and the Prince began to meet one another at sunset by the edge of the forest. Together they settled in the soft grass.

"Look, Tail," Jade said, "the stars are twinkling 'hello'."

"The sky is putting on a wonderful show tonight."

"I love the way the light and air play at nightfall. Why are you so quiet tonight?"

"My mind keeps drifting to the past," sighed the Prince.

"Does it have something to do with the trouble in the forest?" Jade asked.

"I guess so. Let's forget it," he said.

"No," Jade turned and faced him. "Memories are important. They're part of us. Share them with me. You'll feel better."

"I don't want to do that my friend. They're painful."

"It's okay." Jade insisted. "I'm a good listener."

"Are you sure?" Tail tilted his head, his eyes narrowed on her inquisitively.

"Yes," Jade gazed back at him with clear round green eyes.

The Prince took a deep breath and let it out slowly. "Okay, it started when I was about two years old. Butterscotch - a rabbit and my best friend - and I were playing in the woods when she spotted some men working. I wanted to leave, but she insisted on staying. She said we had to care about what the men were doing in our forest and report it to the Elders. It was the first time she ever growled at me, so we stayed. When the men left we went to investigate."

"We sniffed around and found wooden crates with ugly black faces on them. The smell made us gag. It was then that I first spotted the bright pink markers tied around the trees. Butterscotch told me to get one. I never worked so hard to get something. I jumped and ripped at it with my teeth. When I finally got one, it snapped back and hit me. It was my enemy and I didn't know why. We took it with us to show the Elders."

"That was the last time I saw my friend alive. Those markers represented the beginning of painful times. I vowed to remember Butterscotch and take the same path she did - to care about earth and all those who reside here." The fox sighed.

"Go on, Tail," Jade whispered.

"Because of what we found, a meeting of the Elders was held. When it was over there was screaming and howling throughout the forest. Scouts were sent out to find new homes."

"Why did they want to leave the homes they had?" Jade asked.

The fox's face twisted in pain. His tail pounded the ground. A growl rose from deep inside him. "To stay alive, Jade. In less than one turning of the moon, warrens of rabbits fled. Herds of deer vanished. Birds and squirrels abandoned their nests. The bees left their hives. My father moved our den to the golf course."

Jade braced herself and asked what the Humans did.

"First they cut down the forest and took away the trees. Then at dawn, on a chilly morning, my family woke to the ground shaking. The men were using the smelly sticks to explode giant holes in the ground. For weeks the air was black with sick-smelling smoke. And they didn't stop with the forest. The kept blasting, taking up more and more of the Earth."

"I was hunting one night with my brothers. We found a rabbit warren destroyed. It should have been safe. It was part of a cornfield. I found Butterscotch. She was so still."

"I'm sorry," Jade sighed.

"Don't be sorry for me! I've had a good life."

"Is there more?"

"Yes", he said sadly. "Big houses grew out of the holes. Families moved in where our homes used to be. They set up a peaceful community."

"It must have been hard to watch."

"My mother, a wise vixen, told us never to go near people or their houses. She warned us that trusting them would get us hurt. We were young and curious and didn't listen. We'd venture together, a pack of four, Tanner, my older brother, Kip, the baby," the fox softened when he thought of his baby brother, "and Sass my twin sister, who is an Elder now. She saved my life."

"I know Sass. She saved your life! How?" Jade sat up.

"One day when Kip and I were going to play, my Mama said, 'Stay close to home – I feel trouble in the air.' She was so pretty, Jade, the sight of her made you happy. When I tried to tell her not to worry, she smacked my snout. I still remember what she said: 'Don't tell me when to worry, my young Prince. Mind what I say and you'll have no regrets later.'

"Kip and I ran off to find Tanner and Sass. Since Tanner was the oldest, he was in charge and we had to listen to him. Kip never liked that. He used to call Tanner a squirrel head. We found them by a stream, fishing. It didn't take Tanner long to get frustrated because he couldn't catch a fish. He decided we should have a game of chase through the woods. We ran, we hid, and then jumped out trying to scare one another. Before we knew it we were at the other end of the woods near the new development.

'I want to see the children,' Tanner said.

'NO!' Sass growled. Kip and I sat and waited to see who would get their way. Tanner won. He knew she couldn't resist the salty pink meat the children always gave us.

"When we looked out from the edge of the woods, children were there, playing in an open yard. They were delighted to see us. Two of them ran into the house and came out with the meat. What we didn't know was that there were men inside the house.

"The children fed us and in return we let them pet our fur and scratch behind our ears. I guess what happened was, one of the men looked out a window and saw us. When the meat was gone and we started to return to the woods, a voice called to the children. We turned to look. I saw two hunters standing on a deck; their shotguns were aimed at us.

'NO DAD!' a boy screamed. 'RUN,' he cried to us.

"But we were stunned. Shots rang out. Tanner howled. He was hit and died instantly. Kip cried and ran to him. As he stood over Tanner's body, something happened; he looked as if he had been stung by a bee. Slowly, I saw pain move through him, taking his life as it traveled. Finally it took the breath from his mouth. When Kip fell on top of Tanner, Sass dragged me into the woods.

'No Sass,' I cried. 'We have to get Kip and Tanner.'

'They're gone,' was all she said.

"We ran home. But I could never run from any of it. Not the day we lost Tanner and Kip. Or the night I found Butterscotch. And now the markers are back! I've got to stop the madness this time."

He let out a deep howl. His claws dug into the earth.

"We will." Jade promised as she drew in a deep breath. "Your friend George and Love and Man are all going to help."

"I hope they can. You'll get to see George tomorrow night. Jade, I'm suddenly very tired. I think I'll go home."

"I understand." She licked the tears from his snout.

"You know, I do feel better. Lighter. Does that make sense?"

"Yes. Grief and its pain are very heavy."

"Thanks for listening."

When the Prince was gone, Jade looked up at the sky. "Please let this tale have a happy ending," she said to the first evening star.

CHAPTER FIVE

"Jerry… Come on!" Brittany scanned the bushes trying to find the chipmunk. "They're ready to leave."

"I can't do it, Britt," he answered. "I can't walk into your house, climb inside Love's purse, and go off to a town meeting. I'm not that brave."

Jade ran up behind Brittany. "Where is he?"

"In there. He's scared."

"Jerry. Come here," Jade commanded. The little chipmunk appeared and stood on his hind legs. "Are you afraid?"

"Yes, what if they find me, Miss Jade," he whimpered.

"What does Love always do when she catches you?"

"She… she sets me free!"

"She'll take care of you tonight. Don't worry."

"You're right Miss Jade. I'm ready to go."

"Good boy. Let me carry you," Jade said.

The chipmunk lowered his head and lifted his shoulders.

"Brittany, go ahead and make sure our path is clear," Jade said, gently taking the skin of Jerry's neck between her teeth and running to the house.

Once inside they found Love's purse. "Jade, the snap won't open," cried Brittany.

"Watch out. I'll get it." Jade pried the snap open with her teeth. "It's open!"

The chipmunk dove in.

"Here!" Brittany pushed a few tissues on top of her friend.

"Thanks," Jerry said. "What's this? Britt, give me one of your claws." Jerry used the curved nail to open a bag of nuts.

"What are you two doing? Brittany, get out of there!" Jade smacked the young cat on the head. "Jerry, what's that noise?"

"Nothing," answered a muffled voice.

"Be still," Jade hissed, "or you will get caught for sure."

"Looking for something?" Love kneeled down and kissed Jade's head. "Say a pussycat prayer for us to win tonight." Love and Jade shared a hug.

George had been listening and came to her side. "We'll win, pretty lady. Come on, your husband is waiting." Love picked up her purse. Jerry snuggled into a bunch of tissues, and munched on the nuts.

For the next few hours Jade and Brittany waited impatiently with the Prince and Nathanial. The Prince had assigned birds as lookouts along the truck's travel route.

"They have been gone a long time," said Nathanial.

"I hope Jerry didn't get caught," Jade added. "I think he found some food. If he starts chewing…"

The Prince of Tails laughed. "What would your mistress do to him?"

"Bring him home. She likes chipmunks."

"What would she do if you brought me home?" asked the fox.

"I don't know. You wanna find out?"

"You're kidding?"

"Am I?" she purred.

"Here they come," hooted an owl.

Jade and Brittany raced into the house before Love, Man, and George came through the front door. Love left her purse on the dining room table. As soon as the cats were alone, they jumped onto the table.

"Hey Jerry, are you still in there?" Brittany called.

"Jerry, are you all right?" Jade opened the purse, put her head in, and started meowing. "What a mess! Get out of there."

Jerry popped out covered with shredded tissue and pieces of nuts. "Hi! The Land Developer wasn't smiling when the meeting was over. Your Man was brilliant. George chuckled all the way home. We won! I like being a spy," Jerry stated, relieved and proud.

CHAPTER SIX

A few days later Brittany pranced through her country home calling; "Jade, Jade, where are you?"

"Here I am," Jade answered. She was sunning herself under an open skylight in a loft.

"Come outside with me. It's important," Brittany said.

Jade made her way down the steep wooden ladder and followed her sister outside. When she followed Brittany into the woods she was surprised to find several of their friends waiting.

"What's this about?" Jade asked.

"We wanted to thank you, Miss Jade," said Nathanial the woodchuck.

"Look at the trees," Brittany said. As Jade's eyes scanned the forest she realized the pink tree markers were gone.

The Prince of Tails appeared. "We truly won, my friend. How can I ever thank you."

"There's no need," Jade purred, "I love a happy ending."

"She sure does," added Britt the Kit.

Everyone laughed and enjoyed their victory.

The End Of This Sweet Tale

Made in the USA
Middletown, DE
22 April 2015